This book
belongs to:

....

Walnut

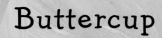
Buttercup

Willow

Lily

Clover

Fern

Acorn

Pip & Spud

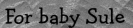

For baby Sule

Scholastic Children's Books
Commonwealth House, 1-19 New Oxford Street
London WC1A 1NU, UK
a division of Scholastic Ltd
London ~ New York ~ Toronto ~ Sydney ~ Auckland
Mexico City ~ New Delhi ~ Hong Kong

First published in paperback in the UK by Scholastic Ltd, 2005

Copyright © Jane Cabrera, 2005

ISBN 0 439 96002 9

All rights reserved

Printed in Singapore

2 4 6 8 10 9 7 5 3 1

The right of Jane Cabrera to be identified as the author and illustrator
of this work has been asserted by her in accordance with the
Copyright, Designs and Patents Act, 1988.

Jane Cabrera's
fairy folk of Leafy Wood

Buttercup's Baby Bird

This is Buttercup
and her friend, Clover.
They are very happy,
for at last spring has arrived
in Leafy Wood.

New life is appearing everywhere!

Out of the soft, warm ground
flowers are popping up
and buds are bursting open
to say hello to spring.

The sky is full of birds singing sweetly
as they collect leaves, soft moss
and twigs to weave into nests.

Looking up at the sky,
Clover giggles,
"Hee hee, look at me!
I'm a bird, too!"

But when he tries to fly,
he falls down with a bump.

Buttercup gives him a cuddle.

Suddenly Clover notices something
falling from a tree . . .

It's an egg!
"Quick, everyone, catch it!"
shouts Buttercup.

The egg lands softly
in the big leaf.

"Come on, Clover,
let's take it somewhere safe,"
suggests Buttercup as they tiptoe
through the dandelions.

They wrap the egg
in leaves and soft moss
to keep it warm and cosy.

Then they sit and they wait
and they wait and they wait
some more, until they hear a small
tappity-tap coming from
inside the egg.

Very soon a baby blackbird appears.
"Tweet, tweet," it chirps hungrily.

"We'll look after you,"
Buttercup and Clover tell the chick,
"and teach you how to fly."

As the days go by,
Little Blackbird grows
bigger and bigger.
Buttercup and Clover teach
her all their favourite games.

But still she cannot fly.

Then one day
Little Blackbird disappears!
Buttercup and Clover look
everywhere for her.

Suddenly they hear singing
way up in the sky and
look up to see . . .

. . . Little Blackbird!
And she's flying!

"Bye, bye, Little Blackbird,"
Buttercup calls.
"See you next spring!"

Walnut

Buttercup

Willow

Lily

Clover

Fern

Acorn

Pip & Spud